Winter Candle

By Jeron Ashford
Illustrated by Stacey Schuett

To Annalyn, Rennie, and Marlise – always share,
And to Chuck, who shares so much.
— Jeron Ashford

To all the Halls – steady lights that they are.
— Stacey Schuett

Book design by Simon Stahl

CIP data for this book is available from the Library of Congress.

Published by Creston Books, LLC
www.crestonbooks.co

Source of Production: Worzalla Books, Stevens Point, Wisconsin
Printed and bound in the United States of America
1 2 3 4 5

Nana Clover checked her list.

Turkey? *In the oven.*
Potatoes? *Peeled.*
Napkins? *Folded, just so.*
Candles?

How could she have forgotten? Thanksgiving at 3C Juniper Court without candles? Unheard of!

Down she padded three flights to the super.

"Candles, Nana C.?" asked Trev. He opened a drawer and handed her a lumpy stick of wax.

"It's not pretty. But it'll burn."

Nana Clover spread some pinecones and leaves around the frumpy candle. By the time her Thanksgiving guests arrived, the centerpiece glowed.

Two weeks later 2G was in an uproar.

"The havdalah candle's not here!" Nat yelled from the closet.

In the kitchen, Mom sighed. "I forgot to buy a new one."

Avi's lip quivered. "But the stars will be out soon!"

"Sha, sha, it's not the end of the world," Grandpa told the Danziger children. "Avi, go ask a neighbor for a candle."

Up Avi clattered and rapped on Nana Clover's door. And down he clumped with the bumpy, drooping candle.

Avi's brothers stared.

"That's not a havdalah candle," Sam groaned. "It's not braided."

"It only has one wick," Nat complained.

"It's not pretty," agreed Grandpa, "but a candle is blessed by what it does, not by how it looks. It'll shine."

And shine it did as Mom raised it high. Grandpa said the blessing to end the Sabbath.

Avi held his hands to the light. They'd never had a havdalah candle that burned so bright.

Four mornings later it was 4D's turn for disaster.

"It's broken!" Kirsten wailed. Liv came running.

One, two, three, four candles on the Saint Lucia crown – and the fifth one snapped in two.

"Our cousins will be here any minute!" said Kirsten. "How can I be Saint Lucia with only four candles?"

Liv started to cry. No St. Lucia crown! And no special Saint Lucia breakfast!

“Girls, we have plenty of time,” Mom reassured them. “Kirsten, go ask a neighbor for another candle.”

Down Kirsten dashed two flights to the Danziger’s—and came back with the funniest-looking candle the girls had ever seen.

“Everyone will laugh at me!” moped Kirsten.

But nobody laughed. Because as Kirsten carried in the teapot and Saint Lucia buns, the funny-looking candle gleamed as brightly as the star of Bethlehem.

Winter came, snow fell, and presents were exchanged. The New Year began. And in 5A, it began with calamity.

"Jamila's got something in her mouth," Donte hollered, "and I don't think it's food!"

Dad scooped up the baby and stuck his finger in her mouth. A piece of wax. A bit of string.

Oh, no!" Donte howled. "Jamila ate the Faith candle for the kinara!"

"Go see if the Ericksons have one," his sister, Monae, suggested.

Down the stairs Donte plodded and knocked on the door.

"You're lucky – we still have this one," Kirsten said. She handed him the bedraggled little candle.

But Donte didn't feel lucky. How could they talk about faith with that sorry thing? And it wasn't the right color!

But when Dad lit the stubby candle, the flame leaped and danced, inviting the other six candles to do the same.

A few days later came the biggest snowstorm of the season. Snow blanketed the front steps and made drifts on the window sills. Then just after nightfall, the electricity went out. Flashlight beams flickered in a few windows.

In 5B, the newest family at Juniper Court huddled together in the dark. Their clothes were still in suitcases. Their dishes were still in boxes. And Papa was somewhere in the city with a moving truck full of furniture.

"How will Papa find us?" Nasreen asked. "The streetlights are out."

"Papa won't find us!" cried Faruq. "There's too much snow!"

"Of course he will find us," Mama said. "Nasreen, go next door and ask the neighbors for a candle. We'll put it in the window to light Papa's way."

Next door Donte scratched his head. "I think there's one left from Kwanzaa," he told Nasreen.

He returned with a lump of wax that looked like a fairy tale troll.

Nasreen's mother lit the candle and set it on the window sill.
"How's Papa going to see one little candle in such a big city?" Faruq asked.

But as they watched, the flame shimmered and grew. It glittered on the falling snowflakes until the dark street seemed spun with stars.

Many blocks away, Papa slowly steered the big truck through snow-covered streets. What did that sign say? Pine Street? Vine Street?

But then Papa noticed a glow up ahead. Maybe someone there could give him directions. Papa steered left, then right, then left. Closer and closer to the glowing light.

Papa turned a corner and gasped.
There in front of him, five stories up,
shone a warm, welcoming light.
He was home!

57TH S
Juniper

Papa climbed three floors, four floors, five floors.

And then –

"Papa's here!" Nasreen and Faruq flew down the hall and into their father's arms.

"Come see our new house, Papa!" cried Nasreen. "And look—everyone else is coming, too!"

The little apartment filled with neighbors. Donte's family brought chairs and a folding table. Nana Clover made a bed out of blankets for Nasreen and Faruq. Trev brought a small heater. The Erickson girls and their mother made sandwiches. And the Danzigers put a pot of soup to warm on the camping stove. Everyone welcomed Nasreen and Faruq and Mama and Papa to their new home.

And the gnarled little candle glowed so brightly in the window that when the electricity finally did come back on, no one even noticed.

Author's Note

Havdalah is a Jewish ceremony to say goodbye to the Sabbath. Families light a special braided candle that has more than one wick so it burns extra-brightly. Havdalah begins when there are three stars in the sky. It ends when the lit candle is dipped in wine and goes out with a sizzle. During Hanukkah, Havdalah is observed before lighting the menorah.

Saint Lucia Day, December 13, is celebrated by Scandinavians in Europe and America. It honors Saint Lucia, who delivered food to the poor wearing a crown of candles on her head to light the way. Today families choose a daughter to be Saint Lucia and carry a delicious breakfast to share with friends.

Kwanzaa is a weeklong celebration at the end of December that honors African culture. African-American families gather to light candles in a kinara, a special candle holder. The candles represent unity, determination, responsibility, cooperation, purpose, creativity, and faith.

Visit your library for more information on these and other special holidays. Go to www.crestonbooks.co for curriculum guides and activities for this book and other Creston titles.